Tag-Along Fred

Kimberly P. Johnson
Illustrated by John Cimino

Visit the author at:
www.simplycreativeworks.com

Pentland Press, Inc.
www.pentlandpressusa.com

Other works by the author:

The Adventures of the Itty Bitty Frog
The Adventures of the Itty Bitty Bunny
The Adventures of the Itty Bitty Spider and the Itty Bitty Mouse
Paperback Poetry – Part I

PUBLISHED BY PENTLAND PRESS, INC.
5122 Bur Oak Circle, Raleigh, North Carolina 27612
United States of America
919-782-0281

ISBN 1-57197-290-0
Library of Congress Control Number: 2001 130298

Printed in China

A Few Words About Kimberly P. Johnson and Her Work. . .

I have read Kim Johnson's delightful stories to my grandchildren, and they loved them!! Her own personality and uplifting spirit are reflected in her stories, and that is good for our children and good for North Carolina.

JAMES B. HUNT, JR.
Governor of North Carolina
1977-1985; 1993-2001

Tag-Along Fred is a wonderful story that expresses the value of town workers with an underlying thread about the self-esteem and self-confidence in young children. Kimberly Johnson does a dynamic job of looking at neighborhood workers through the eyes of a young boy but at the same time creating a character that has loving parents who allow the child the opportunity to grow and explore his world.

Having watched Kimberly Johnson for the past year, I can visualize her telling classes about *Tag-Along Fred*. She displays exuberance for the written word that never fails to get those listening to her excited and involved. This book will add to her growing repertoire of great books for children.

EDNA A. COGDELL
Director of Media Services
Cumberland County Schools

It is with much delight that I extract some thoughts from Kimberly Johnson's new book, *Tag-Along Fred*. As a child, I remember my mom and dad telling me that each person's job was extremely important. They said, regardless of "whether you collect garbage, sweep the floor, sew, teach or whatever you do, give it your BEST." Instilled in me was the sense of purpose, duty, respect and worth. Ms. Johnson has done the same in this rhythmic and diverse book for children and adults. I loved it! Thanks Kimberly! Your job is so important and we appreciate the work that you do to produce quality, age-appropriate, sensitive books.

PAMELA HINES
Manager, PreK-12
University of North Carolina Center for Public Television (UNC-TV)
Research Triangle Park, North Carolina

This book is dedicated to Jeff, my biggest fan: I love you always!! To Charles Smith, my "surrogate" father. To my mom, Susanne, thank you for introducing me to the "real" Tag-Along Fred. You never doubt my abilities; your love and support mean everything to me!! To Fred Rowe, thank you for inspiring this story. You have touched more lives than you will ever know!

"When words are spoken from the heart, they reach out to many people and give them joy. We all have, in our power, the ability to spread joy."

– KPJ

When Fred woke up, it was a beautiful day,
the kind of day that was perfect to play.

Fred told his mom, "I want to make this day as great as it can be!"
She said, "Then find something different to do. It's easy. You will see."

"You can enjoy interesting things, if you take the time and look.
You can draw a picture, write a story or even read a book."

3

"No," said Fred, "I want to do something even more different than that. I'll think of something," he said, as he reached for his hat.

When Fred went outside, the fire truck drove by.
It was shiny and red, with a ladder that reached the sky!

5

The truck stopped near the hydrant, at the end of the street.
Then Mr. Perez stepped down from the driver's seat.

"Hi, Mr. Perez! I'm going to be a tag-along today.
May I tag along with you to see if the hydrants are okay?"

"Sure," said Mr. Perez, "I inspect the hydrants every week
to make sure that we can see them and that they don't have a leak.

You will have to make sure that the reflector is seen at night
and that no trash or grass keeps it hidden from your sight."

"Oh, that's okay, I don't mind."
So, Mr. Perez kept inspecting and Fred tagged along behind.

"Oh, your job is so important and I never really knew
how much we can depend on all the work you do!"

Fred thanked Mr. Perez and waved good-bye.
Then he saw another truck that caught his eye.

This truck was loud as it rumbled down the road.
It was the garbage man, picking up a load.

"Excuse me Mr. Banks, I'm a tag-along today.
May I tag along with you if I stay out of your way?"

"Sure," said Mr. Banks, "my job is hard to do,
but you may tag along with me if you really want to.

Sometimes I pick up bags that aren't always sturdy,
so if you tag along with me, you might get a little dirty!"

"That's okay, I don't mind."
So, Mr. Banks continued working and Fred tagged along behind.

"Oh, your job is so important and I never really knew
how much we can depend on all the work you do."

Then as Fred went home to rest for a minute,
he checked the mailbox to see if mail was in it.

That's when Fred saw Mr. Green walk by.
Mr. Green was the mailman, and he always said "Hi."

16

Fred waved to Mr. Green and he said with a smile,
"I'm a tag-along today, may I follow you for a while?"

"Sure," said Mr. Green, "but I walk a lot each day.
My bag starts out heavy, and gets lighter along the way.

You may have to deliver mail even when the sky is grey
to families and to friends who may live far away."

"Oh, that's okay, I don't mind."
So, Mr. Green walked off and Fred tagged along behind.

"Oh, your job is so important and I never really knew
how much we can depend on all the work you do."

As Fred waved good-bye, he had to cross the street.
That's when he saw the traffic cop. Her name was Mrs. Pete.

"Hi, Mrs. Pete! I'm a tag-along today.
May I tag along with you and help you point the way?"

22

"Sure," said Mrs. Pete, "but there are rules to obey.
Stop, look and listen is what I always say.

You must stand outside in the rain and heat and snow,
so that you can tell others when it's safe to go!"

23

"That's okay, I don't mind."
So, Mrs. Pete crossed the street and Fred tagged along behind.

"Oh, your job is so important and I never really knew
how much we can depend on all the work you do."

When Fred came home, he told his mom and dad what he had learned that day, about jobs and duties and how people earn their pay.

They said, "Every job is important, and we must always remember to be thankful and appreciate all that others do."

26

Mom smiled and said, "I'm glad you did something different, Mr. Tag-Along Fred. After dinner, we'll read a story, then you can tag along to bed!"

The End